Dialogues etc

by the same author

POEMS OF PLACES AND PEOPLE

IN MEMORY OF DAVID ARCHER

for children

THE ALPHABETICAL ZOO

TO AYLSHAM FAIR

Dialogues etc

by

GEORGE BARKER

FABER AND FABER

3 Queen Square London

First published in 1976
by Faber and Faber Limited
3 Queen Square London WC1
Printed in Great Britain by
Western Printing Services Ltd Bristol
All rights reserved

ISBN 0 571 10834 2

© *George Barker, 1976*

What we are dying of, dear Doctor,
  is not the disease:
What we are dying of, dear Doctor,
  is the remedies.

Contents

THE RING-A-ROSES TREE — *page* 11

DIALOGUES OF GOG AND MAGOG: I — 13

AZRAFEL — 14

DIALOGUES OF GOG AND MAGOG: II — 15

TO JOHN BERRYMAN — 17

WE SHALL AT LAST HAVE TIME ENOUGH — 20

THE VELOCITIES OF REMORSE AND LOVE — 21

DIALOGUES OF GOG AND MAGOG: III — 22

MIRANDA — 23

DIALOGUES OF GOG AND MAGOG: IV — 24

EPIGRAM — 26

ON THE BEACH AT FORTE DEI MARMI — 27

DIALOGUES OF GOG AND MAGOG: V — 28

ZENNOR — 29

EVEN VENUS TURNS OVER — 31

LETTER TO A LITERARY FRIEND — 32

DIALOGUES OF GOG AND MAGOG: VI — 34

THE DREAMS OF NIETZSCHE — 36

DIALOGUES OF GOG AND MAGOG: VII — 37

POEM COMPOSED BY AN AGEING APE AT AN IBM
TYPEWRITER — 38

THREE EPITAPHS — 39

THE OAK AND THE OLIVE   42

THE GARDENS OF RAVISHED PSYCHE   44

THE DEATH OF A CAT   45

PASCAL'S NIGHTMARE   46

COLOPHON   48

NEVER A ONE, MY HONEY   49

THE LOVE MACHINE   51

DIALOGUES OF GOG AND MAGOG: VIII   52

THEY BEG FOR LOVE. I ALSO BEG. FOR THEM.   55

The Ring-a-roses tree

What is it that the child
brings to us in both hands
like a bunch of ever
lasting glories or forget me
not that never fade
or daisy chains that net
us all in a ring-a-roses?
It is, I believe, the hope
nothing can extirpate,
that the heart of a stone
still bleeds, still weeps, still
dances along the shore,
still somehow affirms
the metaphysics of dirt,
still feels within the rock
that locked up its own springs
fountains not yet divined.
At the grave of poisoned
intellectual energy
where the intelligence
surrounded with its huge
and hopeless trophies lies,
the cup of suicide still
clutched in a clever hand,
there I have seen the child
step forward, orphaned, and
cast smiling into that grave
its wretched little ring
of rose and daisy. Out
of that overgrown and
undergrowth grave where now
belief and faith like maggots

mock on the rotten bone,
out of that dirt and out
of that stone heart I see
dying upward like hope
the ring-a-roses tree.

Dialogues of Gog and Magog: I

Gog: Where were you when the sun went down
        and the red star arose?
Magog: I was cultivating daisies for
        Posthumous Flower Shows.

Gog: Where were you when the rain began,
        the rain as heavy as blood?
Magog: I was washing from my hands
        the common or garden mud.

Gog: Where were you when the men and women
        and children began to die?
Magog: I was watching from my bedroom window
        with a knowledgeable eye.

Gog: Where were you when four horsemen rode
        out of Apocalypse?
Magog: I lay in bed with a Paddington whore
        counting her umpteen tits.

Gog: Where were you when the angel called
        banging at the door?
Magog: I was too fast asleep to know
        what he was banging for.

        Where were you when they blew my brains
        like eggs out on the bed?
Gog: I was standing with a little gun
        pointed at your head.

Azrafel

When the angel calls somehow we are always
engaged in domestic pursuits of remarkable unimportance
such as polishing the piano top or putting the dog out
or ordering pork chops or strangling a howling baby. For
the powers that be, the angelic authorities, know that
these absurd little human ceremonies comprise the
desperate appeal of our pathos. 'Look,' they whisper,
'see how truly immersed that singular person is in
trying to become two people. Of course he would rather
make love in the kitchen to his second wife than open
the door to an unknown messenger. Who would not sooner
caress the breasts of his wife on her twenty-first birthday
than open the door
to receive a telegram delivered by a glass machine:
"I am the Angel of Death. Refuse to accept this message." '
But then, of course, one day, having nothing better to do,
we open the door.

Dialogues of Gog and Magog: II

Upon a hill I heard them talking
  big Gog and little Magog:
'I thought by now I should know better.'
  Said little Magog to Gog.

'All I know is that the sun rises
  then sets below the tree.
By now I ought to know why this
  odd thing happens to be.'

Said Gog to little Magog,
  'And why me and you?
And what and where and when and how?
  And who my god is who?'

Said little Magog to Gog
  as they looked down at the sea,
'If that's our mother and our father
  what kind of Gogs are we?'

And Gog said to little Magog,
  'I hear a dove in a tree
burbling like a sermonizer.
  But does it hear me?'

Big Gog and little Magog
  stared into each other's eyes
and they saw the sun and the moon and the stars
  like the diamonds of paradise.

'O Gog,' said little Magog,
  'Things all go whence they came.
Let's you and I, my dear friend Gog,
  get up and do the same.'

And little Magog and Gog
  stepped down into the sea
just as if it was god's blue eye
  and they were you and me.

To John Berryman

Let us sit down and speak
briefly about those things
that such men as you
and I have spoken of
since we emerged one dim
and puzzling morning from
the cave of our origins.
I mean not only the
fata morgana and
ambiguous omens of
the red of the sky at dawn
warning the farmer but
Prometheus at dawn
also warning such men
as you and I, for we
too have been forearmed
by fire in the sky
and by the cold wind that
precedes the Eumenides
and heard the thunder over
the horizon turning
the mill stones that grind
so slow, so sure. What was
that word the thunder said?
Nothing. The thunder said
nothing. Nothing.

I have heard the sigh
of Berryman as he
exhaled his everlast-
ing breath and leaped out-
ward and down. That sigh

hangs in the air I breathe
for ever and will hang
over the hill that you
stand on to contemplate
the evening sun that sets
the sky on fire. You
look up and hear it also
the sigh of Berryman falling
upward into the sunset
fires that burn in water
and above agonised Aetna.

The sigh of Everyman!
I have heard it in autumn
evenings full of falling
leaves that burn as they fall,
in the dialogues of dreams
that whisper as they die
and in the flittering of
swallows that foregather
on the wires that measure
how far we are apart,
and in the October burning
of the shorn cornfields as
they crackle into ash and
in the murmuration
of the waterfalling mind
that repeats the same
everlasting sigh of
life that mystifies
itself as it proceeds
continually to die.
The autumn sun is shot
to death with its own gold and
life giving gifts,
and what we die of, love,

is after all a rot
and stuff called living.
Just therefore is the law
that death is what is earned
with every breath we take,
so let us lie down in
its consolatory shade
like workmen who have done
a day's work, and now rest.

We shall at last have time enough

Do not disturb us in the night.
The five signs hang upon the door.
What are you waiting outside for?

Leave us alone to pass the night
as best we may. In this dark room
the inhumed outcome we exhume.

My bones rub yours throughout the night.
I cannot find a decent name
for this love or nothing game.

The little angels in the night
build nests among us, and the moon –
that white-eyed nurse – will leave us soon.

I think that in the silent night
we shall at last have time enough
to speak a little of our love.

The velocities of remorse and love

There are underground passages
in the human psyche that lead
oddly enough, nowhere. They do
so in order to teach us the
existence of the spiritual
void. Thus how can we possibly
love one another? We know from
the disgusting nuptials of
our own double-headed ego
how entirely impossible
this is. And yet love one another
somehow or other we do. What
is the true explanation
of this paradox? It is that
we judge the heart that we know is
rotten with a second heart which
believe it or not we believe
(at its heart of hearts)
is, god help us, not.
For everything we love flies
continually away from
us at a speed of exactly
one hundred and eighty two thousand
regrets per second. And we too
are flying away from what we
love at exactly the same old
guilty spin off. And all, it seems,
simply from shock at finding that
unlike the two hundred lucky
Sophoclean million who didn't,
against all the biological
odds we got ourselves born.

Dialogues of Gog and Magog: III

'To pass the time
the clock ticks continually backward and forward
in front of the ghost,'
sang Gog.
'To pass the time
the ghost walks continually backward and forward
behind the clock,'
sang Magog.
Then they sang together,
'Who walks
backward and forward between the clock and the ghost?'

Miranda

That face of flour with its pale pink and cracked
lips, the eyebrows thin and highly arched and
tinted with gilt and auburn like October fern,
the snaky green eyes glaring or flickering under
a Titian cap of small curls – this face haunts me
and will always haunt me. Loveliest Miranda, was
that a martyrdom of self love or self hate
you so continually and so ostentatiously celebrated?
Endowed with an exquisite taste in
Florentine shoes and nightgowns and victimisations,
whoever practised fellatio with such a ferocious
delicacy, my love, as you?

Dialogues of Gog and Magog: IV

'I was walking,' said Magog, 'in
the fields in the winter when
I heard a fellow singing deep
down in a ditch.
He was shoeless and shapeless and
freezing like an icicle,
he was hungry and thirsty and
he scratched and he itched.'

'He was singing a song about
cherubim and seraphim
and angels in Cadillacs and
archangels so rich
they lit their cigarettes with ten
thousand dollar bills or with
entire forest fires and
they didn't care which.'

'Holy money, holy money,' that
bum sang in his ignorance,
'all the houses of my father are
built with gold bricks,
and the cherubim and seraphim
sit around card tables, all
winning vast fortunes with
three-card tricks.'

'And there when I'm dead I know
that I'll be going, so
I don't at all mind sitting
here in a ditch,
for when I get to heaven, why

every time I'm cold I'll sneeze
dollar bills and diamonds and
Cadillacs and emeralds and
whole showers of fivers till
I'm seriously sick.'

Epigram

When Greek meets Greek a marvellous lie is invented.
When love meets love the Furies stand circumvented.
When ends meet the Archangels rest contented.

On the beach at Forte dei Marmi

On the beach at Forte dei Marmi
yesterday afternoon the Contessa
and I found ourselves with nothing
to do except make love.
I discover that the presence
of a few grains of Italian
sand adds a titillating
piquancy to the act of
heterosexual love.
Until at last the Contessa
turned over, and, leaning
on an elbow as elegant
as a Greek amphora
looked up at me and shook her
silver hair. 'Strawberries,
yes,' she said. 'Cream, yes.
But grains of sand, definitely
no. It feels like
the death of a Thousand
Cuts. Let us return to
a double bed.' 'Contessa,'
I remarked, and taking
her hand drew her down on
the Tyrrhenian sand beside me,
'You will, I hope, remember
that beautiful sentence uttered
by the Archbishop of Toledo
as he pursued up a pillar
in the cathedral a Firbank
catamite he loved:
"Only the oleanders
can ever come between us." '

Dialogues of Gog and Magog: V

'The unhappy are always safe,' said Gog.
   'The eagle lets fall a fatal
turtle upon the bald and well contented head
   and those found dead in ditches
were almost certainly dining with Dionysus.'

'Only the truly unhappy are at liberty,' said Magog,
   'to step blindfold off the pavement
harmlessly into the line of advancing hordes of statistics
   which prove this cannot be done
with complete impunity by any save suicides.'

'But as the comparatively happy lie,' they said together
   'side by side in the spring morning
reading Treasure Island aloud, a ten ton juggernaut lorry
   skids off a cliff overhead and annihilates
those guilty, at that moment, of being happy.'

Zennor

There on the Zennor
moors among old
mineshafts and those
cold villages of
slate and stone and
late flowering gorse
I one after-
noon in May
was walking without
remorse when late as
the day fell I
came upon it, that
small derelict house,
the slate roof caved
in and holly and
hawthorn in-
vesting it all
over wall and window
and dog roses growing
out from under
the kitchen lean to,
and driven downward
through the peeling
unhinged and splintered
door a tree of
bleeding fuchsia
that dripped its
scarlet fragments on
the flag stones and Cain
stained the place
with the crime.
This cottage stood

there with the stake
driven through its
unhinged heart and the
flowers of blood hung and
tinkled to the
small wind like
fuchsia bells and
I knew then that
I had come upon
the death of a
small home which
had drawn this heart
transfixing murder
into and out
of itself.

Even Venus turns over

When frogs dream do they also dream that they have
forgiven themselves and turned back into tadpoles?
Yes, to pity is to assume a dream of
the seeming demigod. But this is not merely a 'seeming'.
Are we truly superior to those whom we pity because
at that moment, we believe, we are not also degraded
by the dirty snot rag? At the night of love
even Venus turns over in her sea blue bed
so that she can be buggered. The derelict
church stands empty on the little hill
and over it clouds of cherubs play water polo
with the head of St Paul. These emotions resemble
an empire over which the cadent moon of pity
is always setting. They seem, like volcanic islands,
to get born in a single convulsive moment, but
unlike those dead islands, they never die.

Letter to a literary friend

You ask me, frivolously, to send you reminiscences.
What you do not know is that I can in truth recall
nothing whatsoever of those days. All the happy
apparitions have been exorcised, all the debaucheries
have been, I believe, expiated; all the assassinations
exonerated and those who died have, to a man, been
immured with appropriate ceremonies of farewell.
Let the dead speak and so on. But if you ask me
what, if anything, I have derived in the way of
knowledge of you or myself, what insight into affairs,
or in the way, god help us, of commonplace wisdom,
how can I answer? A finicky and whimsical
picking and choosing of events and memories
wholly foregone, the scribbling of jokes and anecdotes
in parallel lines and the recital of them
to three friends over a fire in the autumn evening
this is, I know, a harmless and charming pastime.
But I would not wish to do this. I think it
a rather hypocritical dishonouring of the events
and of the men who helped to construct the
untriumphal Arch of Life. They deserve something
better than to be versified. Might they not well
be left in the peace and whatever of spiritual
dignity we retain in the grave? Only
logomachic vulgarians would choose to prod these and
suchlike corpses with an indexing finger or
disturb their posthumous serenity, so hardly
won, with the chattering of etymologies, or
the contemptible necrology of memory. My friend,
if from the grave I could raise up even
the least of these dead, these defected corpses,
you might well find your hand as you extended it

burn like five Roman candles. Not because all
heroes are, of course, dead but because of
the law of diminishing returns. What things call for
now (and a serpentine voice they call in) seems to be
simply the faculty of disguise. One does one's best
to look like someone or something else in order
to evade the consequences of having in fact done so.
And the person we have become is the man whom
we always hated, the one who won, the Victor Vae
Ludorum. I stand around with the silver cup in my hands
and I am just a little shocked to find it contains
nothing but cyanide.

Dialogues of Gog and Magog: VI

'The history of man', said Gog,
    'is like a bloody sack
full of old rags and bones, which
    I carry on my back.

'It is so heavy that I feel
    as if I was a snail
with the dead giant Consequence
    sitting on my tail.

'I cannot even take time off
    as in my bog I sit
without it smothering me as
    I take a simple shit.

'I wish,' Gog said, 'that I was not
    an ordinary man
for then I would regret it all
    ever since Time began.

'I see no purpose in the stones
    that spin around the sky
and even less in the vision that
    hallucinates my eye.

'I think that I will lie down and
    begin to dream a dream
where nothing ever happens or
    even seems to seem.

'I will undream my soul who sits
   on a big summer cloud
wrapped up in last week's laundry like
   a penitential shroud.

'I will undream America
   and Euston Railway Station;
I will undream Psychology and
   universal creation.

'I will undream the love I made
   in beds I never shared:
I'll watch it turn back into sperm
   then into MC^2.

'I will undream the Seven Seas
   and all the little fishes,
I will undream all that came true
   of all the wicked wishes.

'I will sit down and undream it all
   till nothing's left whatever,
and it will seem as though nothing was
   and never had been. Never.'

The dreams of Nietzsche

I

Those hopeless spirits, they fall from planet to planet
and in the circle of absence lament the home
they have forgotten. Do the gods remember
that when they constructed the existential machine
they found that they were compelled to build themselves
as their own victims into it? Those hopeless spirits
they fall from planet to planet and in the circles
of space lament the home they have forgotten.

II

I see them playing and splashing in the gold baths of the sun
the cherubs whom no one has as yet called to step
down here howling. They disport themselves with fiery
     atoms and
balls of rainbowing molecules and performing salamanders
and pyromaniac godfathers. Dripping with fire they fly
abstractly chanting of times to come when perhaps they
     will find
that paradise to which above all else they aspire, the bosom
of the one who loves them so much that she calls them down
out of the golden baths of the sun and rainbowing molecular
     games
to weep themselves asleep in the cold cradles of the clay.

Dialogues of Gog and Magog: VII

Beside the Wensum river Gog and Magog sat fishing
one Wednesday morning in April when the water was
so like a well-washed looking glass they could not help
    reflecting:
'Who are those two beautiful people staring up at us?'

And two birds of dawning descended and sat upon their
    shoulders
and the birds stared down into the river as it ran:
'Who are those beautiful birds that lie sleeping in the river?
They cannot be us,' they said. 'But then again, they can.

'For early in the morning when the dew hangs from the
    railings
and the sun walks up from the bedrooms of the sea
we step out of our dreams having bathed in such waters
that we rise up like the dayspring as clear as can be.

'O somewhere near midnight and through mirrors of seeming
beyond the doors of nightmare, and the madhouse of heaven,
there must be a fountain in whose glittering lustrations
yesterday is justified, and even forgiven.'

Poem composed by an ageing ape at an IBM typewriter

The burden of the unintelligible world is
not, to me, its unintelligibility, it is my
ineradicable and natural conviction that
the operation of stars must, in the end,
make – well, a little sense. What happens when I spend
my life contemplating a meaningless and therefore
unanswerable conundrum? I grow daily
more and more certain it foreshadows an answer
but is there a cipher that conveys no message?
I suspect that the only communication
possible between primates is conveyed via
the emotion evoked by images and that all
intellectual operations fail at heart to communicate
anything whatsoever. Why did Piero
della Francesca abandon painting and
devote himself at last to mathematics? For
the same reason as he painted his Ideal City
as a place without people. The memories
that go to make up or construct the museum
of the imagination possess the rather
frightening ability to break out of
their glass cases and run riot throughout
the intellectual corridors. What they are trying
desperately to find is the home
of a world that remains, thank god, unintelligible.

Three epitaphs

At the death of this Austrian chorister
   did the chorus of cherubim
suddenly hear their canticles grow more melodious
   simply because of him?

Down here the ugly ducklings and the dumb
    Miltons and phoney Ophelias
wait, Miss Smith, to hear your beautiful voice
    join with St Cecilia's.

Hitherto I have wasted a lot of time and words
  eulogising the life and death of my friends.
The least I can do for myself is the least I can do
  to make amends.

The oak and the olive

Seven years lived in Italy leave me convinced
that the angel guarding us knows only too well
what she is doing. There is a curious sense
in which that place whose floral sophistication
– whose moral sophistication – we all happily acknowledge,
resembles in fact a delicious garden inhabited
by seven-year-old children. I can perceive
this innocence of spirit even in the most cynical
of Italians I have loved, and I think that
this innocence ensues simply from the sun. There
it is perfectly possible to assassinate one's best friend
with a kind of histrionic guiltlessness, because
the sun would continue to shine after the crime,
the gardens to dream in the afternoon, and later
the evening cast a benevolent shadowing over
the corpse of one's cold friend. Furthermore years
of white and gold sunlight tend to deprive one of
the pessimistic faculty. It is harder to indulge there
the natural Anglosaxon melancholy
because I, for instance, found a bough of oranges
growing through the skylight of my lavatory.
And all these mother of pearl evenings and these
serene Venus green skies and Lucullan landscapes
have in the end the effect of depriving one
of precisely that consciousness of shame out
of which the adult Nordic monster
of evil is generated. There are no Grendls here.
And so it is possible often in the Borghese
Gardens to act as though one was, of course,
a criminal cynic but a criminal cynic whom
the sun does not decline to befriend, to whom small
birds still confide, and whom the sylvan

evening landscape is still prepared to sleep with.
Then it seems likely that Providence or Italy or
even the conscience has forgiven us the enormities
that brought us here. When the chilling
rain falls upon me in the North I know
only too well that it does so as
a moral punitive. I write this in
a Norfolk August and the rains pour down
daily upon a landscape which derives
its masculine nobility from the simple
fact that it has survived. It has survived
the flood, the winter, the fall and the Black
nor'-easter. The old oak tree hangs out
that great twisted bough from which the corpse
of the criminal cynic has just dropped in decay.
The clouds do not decorate the sky, they entomb it,
and the streams have swollen to cataracts. Weeds
flourish and the summer corn is crushed flat.
What could ever come from all this hopeless
melancholy save a knowledge, as by allegory,
of our culpability? Why, then, should I find
a child's face bright with tears haunting my mind?

The gardens of ravished Psyche

Do not speak to us of dreams, speak to us of autumn in
the gardens of ravished Psyche where the golden haired
      laburnum
has long since burnt itself to ashes and the old apple tree
stands blackened and rotten and the ground around it lies
covered with dead fruit and the salt of the dead sea.

Now those arbours are forsaken and the trellis vines
      decaying;
the rats huddle and nibble in the skulls of the demigods;
the lake has taken wing and the lovers have forgotten
why they were born, and the golden apples from the branches
have long since fallen, my love, long since fallen.

The death of a cat

No, it was nothing much. Just the ginger
cat lying poisoned among ancient rusting
farm machinery in the stable, his pale blue
and gentle eyes filmed over and disgusting.

I cannot suppose his death has been recorded
in the heavenly archives but here in this
old house it certainly has been, simply because
if possession's nine points of the law, well, it was his.

Yes, this old farmhouse truly belonged to him: when,
six years ago a family came to this place
on a day of tumultuous rain and exhausted children and cold
winds as hostile as a spit in the face,

then, when, expecting little, we opened the door,
sitting up there in the hall, as small as a mouse,
this ginger kitten looked at us, turned, and then
led us like a walking welcome into the house.

A couple of years ago he was caught up
in a wire gin trap for a fortnight and more.
He lost a back leg. So he hunted on three.
(I hope he does so somewhere else on four.)

No, it is nothing much. The ginger cat
is dead, and buried. But then again, I see
those beautiful eyes occluded with a poison that
one day, my friend, may infect you, and me.

Pascal's nightmare

I see them flickering
in shadows and painted
flames, the wry-necked
executives and hairy
con men, the strumpets
rubescent, the pornos
weary of fucking, the
visions with golden
locks staring into
cracked lenses, and contra-
ceptives everywhere jerking together like water pumps
and the hissing and
sighing and kissing of
all the exhausted
egos beckoning in these
shadows. I see faces
wearing old masks of scorched
skin and meat, green eyes
envying without pity
others who burn and
flaunt in their
self love like the
torches of Nero. The
electric machines sit
around, cross legged,
sipping iced glasses of
Nietzsche's tears, and a
bald headed vulture
hopping and flapping and
flouncing from bed to
bed silently lugs

in its dead claws
like a rag doll the
burning babe of a
normal abortion in
christening robes from
chair to mantel
piece and from bed to fire
place around the
room. The silence
of the dead appals me.
Still sleeping in
their deep geological
beds the children of
unborn Urania beg to
be left to their dreams.
And out of an empty sky
useless rain falls for
ever down and down
through the silent spaces
of Pascal's nightmare.

Colophon

'To purify the dialect of the tribe'? And why?
So that we can direct against the Head Hunter
a last and truly lucid diatribe?

Never a one, my honey

Never a one, my honey,
Never a one will come
back through the door of roses
in the bright morning from
those beds of Remember
where like the stars or strangers
they sleep so long alone.

Never a one, my honey,
never a one will call
not though the clock strikes midday
there on the kitchen wall;
never a one will answer
no matter how you call,
never a one will come, my honey,
never a one at all.

Not the blonde milkmaid with her
face like a cherubim
and an old milkjug full of
poison to the brim,
she will not come again, my honey,
and knock upon the door
and weep a couple of glass tears
down on the kitchen floor.

Nor will the bedtime sailors
who sleep in the Russian sea
get up and walk the water
back to you or me;
and the nights will cover over
all the girls in black

and never a one, my honey,
never a one will come back.

The birds and bees and flowers
yes, every bloody thing
will come and gawp through the window
some morning in the spring.
But they will not come, my honey,
no matter how you call
never a one will come, my honey,
never a one at all.

The love machine

The star that I was born under
declines to acknowledge its paternity.
The children I played with by the Thames
continue to play in Battersea Park
disguised, all of us, as memories.
They hang around the gates of eternity.
For I am an inventor
who has only just failed to
mutate himself into
a machine capable
of manufacturing that enormity:
artificial love.

Dialogues of Gog and Magog: VIII

'Good morning, Gog,' I said.
  'What are we doing today?'
'Listening to our hearts,' he said,
  'beating the time away.'

'That's not the heart,' I answered,
  'you hear tick and knock.
It's my sympathetic nervous system
  or the old cuckoo clock.'

'All that you have inside your
  hairy chest,' he said,
'is that old cuckoo clock and it
  ticktocks until you're dead.'

'Indeed, indeed,' says I, 'and that
  may very well be so
but when it stops where does my little
  my poor little cuckoo go?'

'The cuckoo to Cloud Cuckooland
  ups, then, and takes wing
to that far home from home where no
  alarm clocks ever ring.

'There there is no sun arising
  or circles of the moon,
there is no kiss in the morning
  and no gun at noon.

'There is no river running
  into a future tense;

and long though you look down, it
   bears no image hence.

'There is no sighing for the
   love that you may find
around the corner because there
   all the corners are blind.

'There is no breaking of the
   brachiolated heart,
where what has grown together is
   tomorrow torn apart.

'There is no circumambu-
   lation of the stars
as superior to us as
   millionaires' motorcars.

'But there the sun is always
   high in the empty sky;
no future casts a shadow into
   the blue and present eye.

'The kingfisher's transfixed in
   the rainbow of his sweep –
the sleeping willows never
   waken up to weep.

'There in the morning gardens
   the children of the clay
have charmed the time out of the clock
   and never age a day.

'The waves are always breaking
    although they never break
and the footprints of the wind have gone
    from the surface of the lake.

'There the suns hang for ever
    in the eternal tree.
— The cuckoo will never call again
    for you, my love, or me.'

They beg for love. I also beg. For them.

How can I see them? Part of them is me.
They will not answer when I ask their names.
Sometimes I do not know if they are even here
When I perceive them. I am their knowledge of
Their own identity, because the purpose
Of my half existence is to elicit theirs.
They beg for love. I also beg. For them.